NEEDY BITCH

A SHORT STORY

ALEXANDRIA BLAELOCK

BlueMere Books

MELBOURNE, AUSTRALIA

For permission requests, please contact
enquiries@bluemerebooks.com.

Ordering Information:
Discounts are available on quantity purchases. For details, contact orders@bluemerebooks.com.

Needy Bitch/Alexandria Blaelock
paperback ISBN: 978-1-925749-32-8
digital ISBN: 978-1-925749-33-5

Book Layout © BookDesignTemplates.com

NEEDY BITCH

J ust before dawn, the sun limped through the guest room curtains casting shadows of light across the room.

Outside, a chorus of kookaburras and magpies greeted the day.

It was beautiful, yet poignant, as if they knew the house was in mourning.

Sam closed her eyes against the tears and wondered how she'd ever slept through it.

She heard a slight whimper and rolled over to look at the needy bitch who'd been sharing her bed. With her big brown eyes, elfin features and golden hair, Sam hated her with a passion.

And hated herself for hating Daisy.

For all she knew, Daisy might miss Max more - her neediness more about comfort and connection than being the naturally bossy and demanding dog she was.

Daisy opened her eyes and thumped her tail heavily on the bed; once, and after a pause, once more.

Sighing, Sam reached out to scratch her behind the ears, just where she liked it. She wasn't Max, but her soft doggy body was warm and comforting.

Alive. As well as next to her.

Daisy rolled on her back, exposing her belly, and Sam shifted her scratching attention there. The stink of warm dog made the day seem normal and somehow manageable.

Hopefully, it'd be a good day; she'd get something done, and Daisy would eat a little more and cling a little less.

Not that Daisy hadn't been clingy all her life, but without Max's balancing influence, having her around was like having an ear infection.

It hurt, and no matter how much you scratched it, it was never enough.

When a Labrador stops eating, you can't help but worry.

Especially when that Lab had never missed a meal.

And loved going for walks because she could scarf up discarded sandwiches, fallen fruit and possum poo before anyone else noticed it was there.

Who made them cut a beach holiday short because she'd eaten something and spent a day and a night throwing up.

Sighing again, Sam crawled out of bed, dragged Max's robe around her and went to the kitchen.

She scrubbed her dry, gritty eyes with the heels of her palms, and drank a half-empty leftover bottle of beer.

With tail half-mast and a scrabble of claws, Daisy arrived in the kitchen.

"Hey Daisy."

Morning routine dictated Daisy receive a big hug and a back massage before being let out to perform her toilette.

It was warmer outside than in her heart, so Sam left the door open, and from habit, started preparing two cups of coffee.

Not that the hot, bitter drink would make up for another mostly sleepless night, but the routine, led into other routines, and sometimes she got through the day.

The percolator clicked and hissed, as she stared out the window - curtains still open from whenever she'd opened them last.

As the perfume of coffee filled the air, Daisy arrived back and grunting, settled on the floor.

Habit required emptying the dishwasher. Sam smiled grimly at the bleakness of a dishwasher filled with ones. One pot, one plate, one mug.

It was the exercise of loneliness; bend, reach, stand, stack - five repeats ladies!

Catching sight of the two mugs brought tears to Sam's eyes once more, and she groped in her pockets for a tissue. When all she came up with was a crumpled mass of torn tissue paper, it was too much, and she couldn't hold the sobs in any longer.

She crouched protectively as the pain hit, crying hard, body wrenching sobs.

Max was never coming back.

His memory saturated the house, from the run-down shack they'd bought and renovated, to the antiques they'd scoured markets for, to the canvases he'd painted himself.

After a point, her breathing evened out, and she noticed her knees ached.

She stood, wiping her nose and face on the robe's hem.

Everyone said it would get easier. All she had to do was survive, one minute at a time.

Habit made her pour two coffees.

Habit usually made her take them back to bed with Max, but their room was as he'd left it on the last day.

If only she'd known it would be the last day.

Instead, she took both mugs to the table, placing one in front of his empty chair. As she sat, clasping her mug in both hands, regarding his empty seat, she couldn't help thinking about all the promises they'd made each other about what the future would bring.

So much for together forever.

She took a sip of hot coffee.

"I'm so angry at you right now," she said. "How could you just leave me like this?

"You just left, you didn't even say goodbye.

"You never even once looked back, just ran on ahead without me."

As the tears started flowing again, Daisy lumbered over and leaned comfortingly against her leg.

Sam scratched the dog's head as she addressed her dead husband.

"You didn't even make any preparations - you left it all to me.

"How am I supposed to get my head around it all when I don't know anything about it?"

Sam reached out towards him, as if he would take her hand and apologise.

Or more likely, laugh at her irritation and make some kind of joke.

He'd never taken life too seriously.

"What am I supposed to do without you?

"I hate you..." She sniffed and took a long gulp of her coffee.

"I love you; I can't live without you."

She tried to imagine what he would say in reply.

"For heaven's sake woman, you're a mess, pull yourself together.

"Why don't you take a shower once in a while and wash your hair?

"And for god's sake, eat something. You and Daisy both - you need to take better care of my girl Daisy."

Sam smiled a little sadly; she sounded just like him.

Max wasn't much of an apologist. He left the past in the past and moved on.

Not asking for permission or apologising for the things he could control let alone those he couldn't change.

Nothing much you can change about dying.

But imaginary Max was right, Sam wasn't exactly sure when she'd last bathed, and she really should make more of an effort to eat whether she felt like it or not.

She'd need her strength.

She drained her coffee, hauled herself into the ensuite, and rooted around the cupboard looking for that fancy body wash he'd bought her for Christmas. Daisy settled on the bath mat to watch.

Sam washed her hair and scrubbed her body before rubbing herself dry with a towel that needed washing too.

Ignoring the unmade bed, she pulled on clean jeans that were too loose, and one of his t-shirts.

Imaginary Max wolf-whistled.

Daisy followed Sam back to the kitchen and watched her pour dog biscuits. She sat and looked back at Sam witheringly.

Sam checked the fridge for something else that might tempt the dog but was just shuffling expired food from one place to another.

She dragged the bin over and started throwing the rotten food into it. In the end, the fridge was empty bar milk, half a carton of eggs, an unopened packet of Gruyere, and half a jar of kimchi.

Imaginary Max raised one eyebrow quizzically.

A cheese omelette would do, and given Daisy liked eggs and cheese, perhaps she'd eat some too.

Sam cracked a couple of eggs into a bowl and whipped them, then opened the cheese and grated some onto a plate, before sitting on her haunches and offering the dog a few grates.

Daisy regarded her steadily, so she nibbled at the cheese before offering it again, and this time the dog took it.

Sam heated a fry pan and added the eggs. While they cooked, she prepared coffee for one. When the eggs were almost done, she added the cheese and folded the omelette then poured the coffee.

And a minute later, slid the omelette onto a plate.

As Sam carried breakfast to the table, she imagined Max applauding.

She'd already achieved more this morning than any other day since he'd gone.

She settled in her chair and prepared to cut into the omelette.

Daisy strolled around the table, sat in her line of sight looking up at her

And as Sam started eating, Daisy began drooling.

After a couple of mouthfuls, Daisy whined a breathy whine and scooted a little closer. And after another couple, Daisy put her head in Sam's lap.

Sam smiled and brushed the dog's head with one hand. Then she put the plate on the floor, and Daisy was on it in an instant.

Another small achievement.

Bathed, dressed and dog fed.

Now it was time to do something about getting back to normal.

Well, not back to normal; with Max gone, things would never be back to normal.

But it was time to let him go and work with Daisy to create a new kind of normal.

THE END

ABOUT THE AUTHOR

Alexandria Blaelock writes stories, some of them for *Ellery Queen's Mystery Magazine* and *Pulphouse Fiction Magazine*. She's also written four self-help books applying business techniques to personal matters like getting dressed, cleaning house, and feeding your friends.

As a recovering Project Manager, she's probably too fond of sticking to plan. She lives in a forest because she enjoys birdsong, the scent of gum leaves and the sun on her face. When not telecommuting to parallel universes from her Melbourne based imagination, she watches K-dramas, talks to animals, and drinks Campari.
At the same time.

Discover more at www.alexandriablaelock.com.

OTHER SHORT STORIES BY ALEXANDRIA BLAELOCK

Kiss of Death
Long Weekend in the Snow
Shining Star
Phoenix Child
Ship in a Bottle
Lady of the Looking Glass
Simone Says Hands in the Air
Life in the Security Directorate
Fate in Your Hands
Love in the Security Directorate
Alma's Grace
Payton's Run
The Guardian's Vigil
The Life and Death of Carmelita Basingstoke
Balancing the Book

BOOKS BY
ALEXANDRIA BLAELOCK

Stress Free Dinner Parties
Build Your Signature Wardrobe
Holistic Personal Finance
Ms Blaelock's Book of Minimally Viable
Housekeeping